Plum
and
Rabbit
and
Me

Emma Chichester Clark

HarperCollins *Children's Books*

First published in paperback in Great Britain
by HarperCollins Children's Books in 2010

ISBN-13: 978-0-00-727325-6

10 9 8 7 6 5 4 3 2 1

HarperCollins Children's Books is a division of HarperCollins Publishers Ltd.

Visit our website at: www.harpercollins.co.uk

Printed in China

I have a little sister called **Plum**.
She is *okay*,
sometimes.

But, she **follows** me around,

and she copies me.

And she **takes** **my** things.

I have to let her, because
she is smaller than **me**.

But I get them back
because
they're mine.

One day,
   Granny gave me a book,
and Plum...

a rabbit.

I didn't want the book.
I wanted the **rabbit**.
"It's not fair!"
I said to Mum.

Plum wouldn't
let me hold it.

I gave her my old penguin,

      but she wouldn't let me have the **rabbit**.

I gave her my elephant with three legs,

      but she **still** wouldn't let me have it.

I gave her my
old squashy frog
with one eye,

and my
second-best
football.

"Now, can I have it? I said,
and she said,

"No! My wabbit!"

So, I hit her...

my room!

up to

and ran

...and I took the rabbit,

I could still hear
Plum screaming
when I shut the door.
It went **on**
and **on,**

and then I heard Mum...
coming up the stairs.

I pushed the rabbit under my bed.

"Hello, Mum!"

I said.

"I am
not at all pleased
with you, Humber,"
she said.

"But it's not **fair!**"
I said.

"It's **not** fair
to hit your little sister,
is it?"
asked Mum.

"And it's not fair
        that you have **all these toys,**
and she hardly has **any,** is it?"
        asked Mum.

"And if you got a new toy,
how would you like it if Plum took it?"
asked Mum.

"She does take my toys," I said.
"But she gives them back," said Mum.
"Well, I'm going to give it back!"

I said.

"Are you?" asked Mum.
"Because if not,
you could give her this old bear..."

I thought she was joking,
but she picked up my bear,
and took it
downstairs!

I think she was just about
to give him to Plum,
but I got there **first**.

"Here you are, Plum,"
I said.
I gave her the rabbit.

"Now can I have
   my bear back?"
I said.

"What else are you
   going to say to Plum?"
Mum asked.

"I'm sorry, Plum,"
I said.

"Well done, Hum!"

said Mum.

Have you read all the stories about Humber and his sister Plum?

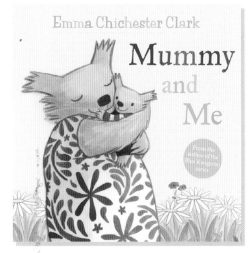

Humber and Plum — Mummy and Me
978-0-00-727323-2 • paperback £5.99

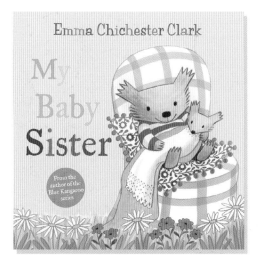

Humber and Plum — My Baby Sister
978-0-00-727324-9 • paperback £5.99

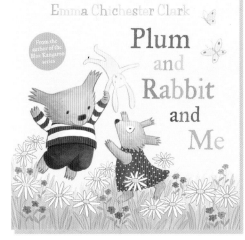

Humber and Plum — Plum and Rabbit and Me
978-0-00-727325-6 • paperback £5.99